# The Journey of
# OLIVER K. WOODMAN

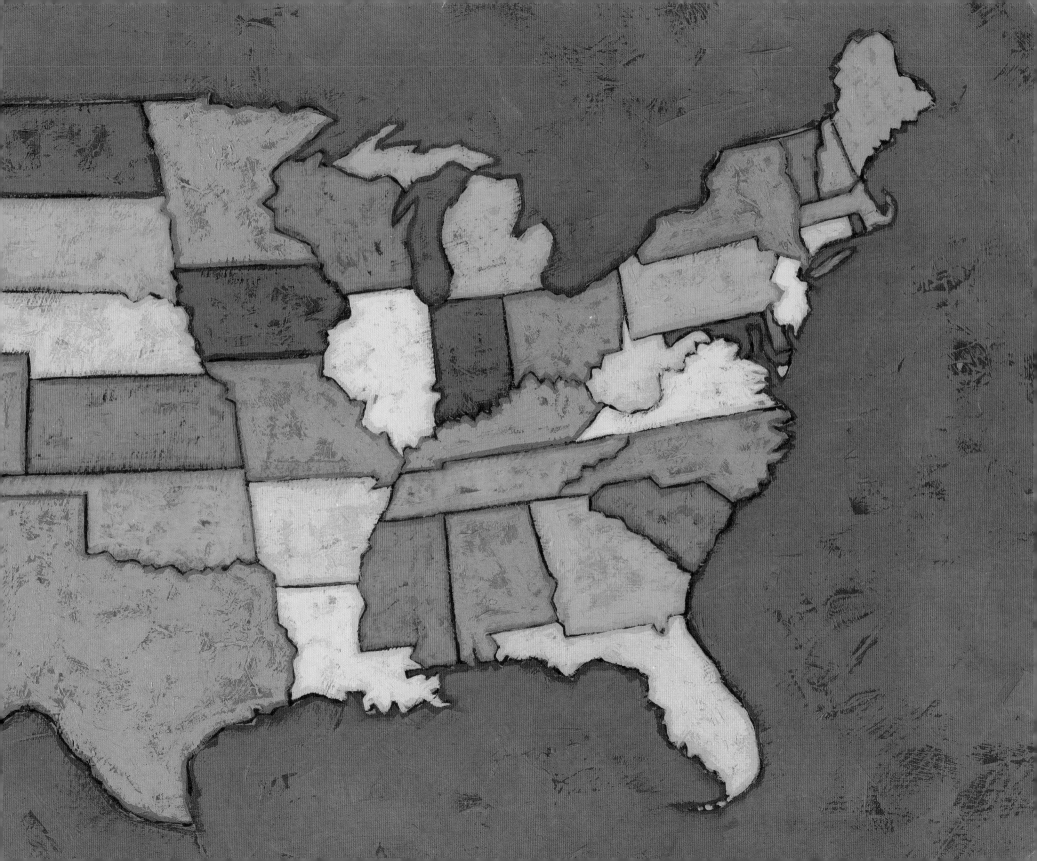

# The Journey of

WRITTEN BY **Darcy Pattison**

ILLUSTRATED BY **Joe Cepeda**

# OLIVER K. WOODMAN

sandpiper

**Houghton Mifflin Harcourt**

**Boston New York**

All rights reserved. Published in the United States by Sandpiper,
an imprint of Houghton Mifflin Harcourt Publishing Company,
Boston, Massachusetts. Originally published in hardcover in the
United States by Harcourt Children's Books, an imprint of
Houghton Mifflin Harcourt Publishing Company, New York, 2003.

SANDPIPER and the SANDPIPER logo are trademarks of
Houghton Mifflin Harcourt Publishing Company.

Requests for permission to make copies of any part of the work
should be submitted online at www.harcourt.com/contact or
mailed to the following address: Permissions Department,
Houghton Mifflin Harcourt Publishing Company,
6277 Sea Harbor Drive, Orlando, Florida 32887-6777.

www.sandpiperbooks.com

The illustrations are in oils over an acrylic under-painting on board.

The Library of Congress has cataloged the hardcover edition as follows:
Pattison, Darcy.
The journey of Oliver K. Woodman/Darcy Pattison; illustrated by
Joe Cepeda.
p.    cm.
Summary: Oliver K. Woodman, a man made of wood, takes a
remarkable journey across America, as told through the postcards
and letters of those he meets along the way.
[1. Dolls—Fiction.    2. Travel—Fiction.    3. Postcards—Fiction.
4. Letters—Fiction.]    I. Cepeda, Joe, ill.    II. Title.
PZ7.P27816Jo    2003
[E]—dc21        2001005320
ISBN 978-0-15-202329-4
ISBN 978-0-15-206118-0 pb

Manufactured in China
SCP 10 9 8 7 6 5 4 3 2 1

For Dwight
—D. P.

For that seventeen-year-old boy
with an undaunted spirit of adventure,
who left home twenty-five years ago
and faced the world
—J. C.

May 10
Redcrest, CA

Dear Uncle Ray,
    Please come to visit us this
summer.
    We will go camping. We can swim
and catch fish.
    You are my favorite uncle.
Please say you will come!

        Love,
        Tameka
        XOXOXO

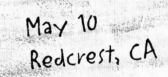

May 17
Rock Hill, SC

Dear Tameka,
   I'd love to come to California,
but I can't. I will be building
kitchen cabinets for some
new apartments all summer.
   But maybe my friend Oliver
will come to visit!

Love,
Uncle Ray

Dear Traveler,

I am going to see Tameka Schwartz, 370 Park Avenue, Redcrest, California, 95569. Please give me a ride and help me get there. If you don't mind, drop a note to my friend Raymond Johnson, 111 Stony Lane, Rock Hill, South Carolina, 29730. He wants to keep up with my travels.

Thanks,
OLIVER K. WOODMAN

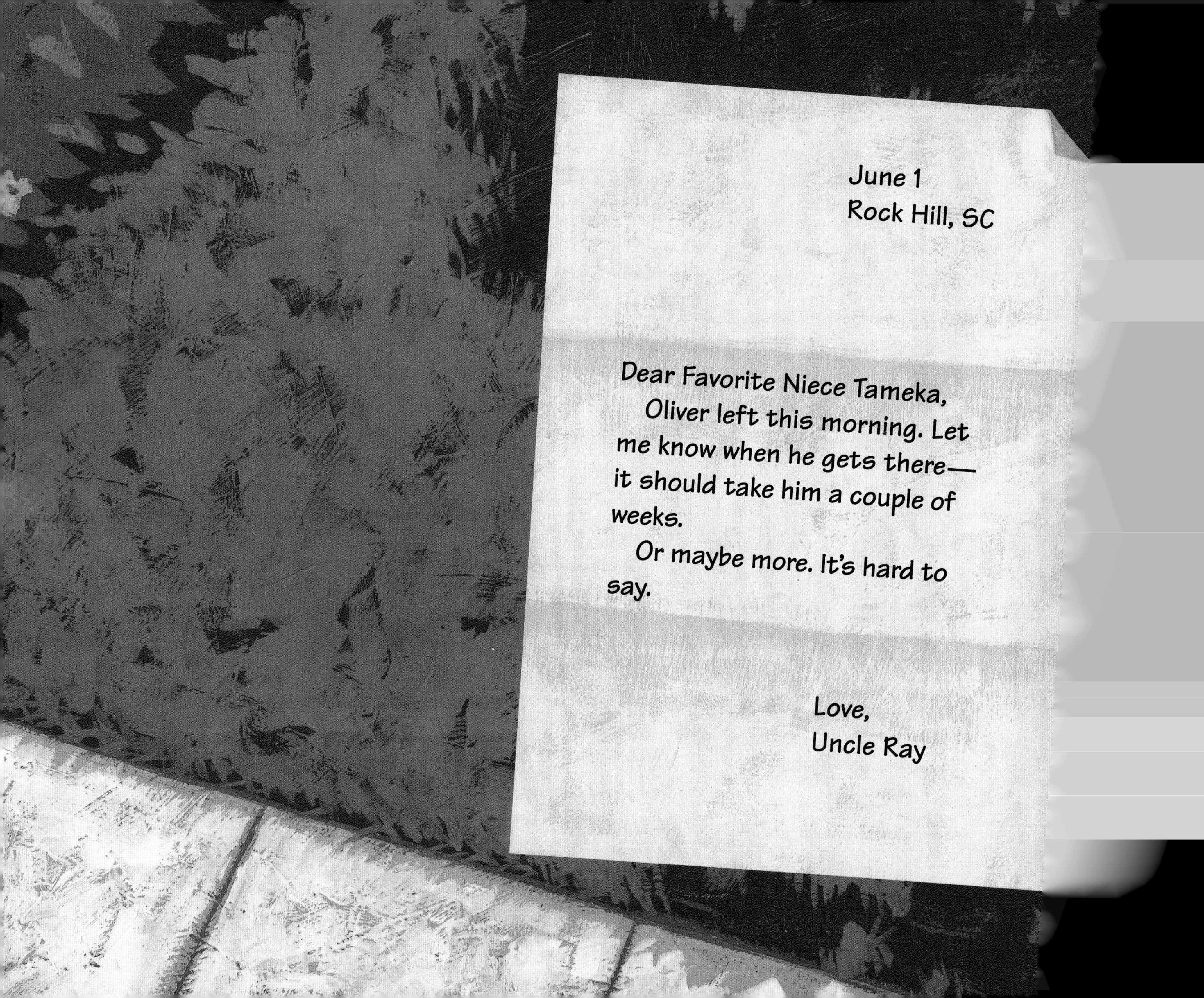

June 1
Rock Hill, SC

Dear Favorite Niece Tameka,
   Oliver left this morning. Let me know when he gets there—it should take him a couple of weeks.
   Or maybe more. It's hard to say.

Love,
Uncle Ray

June 4
McTavish Plantation
Outside Memphis, Tennessee

Dear Ray:
  For two days, Oliver rode in the back of my truck and kept Bert, my Brahman bull, company. I delivered Bert to his new home and he's settling in, but he'll miss the late-night conversations and singing with Oliver.
  I left Oliver east of the Mississippi River, just outside Memphis, and hurried home to my beloved Amelia.

                    Yours truly,
                    Jackson McTavish

June 8
Forrest City, AR

Hi! Mr. OK is OK. Quinn and Sherry went to a basketball game at The Pyramid in Memphis, Tennessee, last weekend and brought Mr. OK back. He hung out with us for a couple of days, and all the girls liked him better than Quinn. So when Quinn's cousin's boyfriend's aunt was leaving to visit her sick grandfather in Fort Smith, Arkansas, the guys loaded Mr. OK into the aunt's station wagon and sent him on his way. We didn't even get to say good-bye!

Cherry (Sherry's sister),
for the Gang

P.S. If you see Mr. OK again, tell him we all said good-bye.

Raymond Johnson
111 Stony Lane
Rock Hill, SC 29730

June 11
Albuquerque, NM

Hey, Ray—
    I drive a moving van for Southeast Moving Company. I picked up Oliver at the Arkansas border, then drove west to Oklahoma City, Oklahoma, south to Dallas, Texas, northwest to Amarillo, Texas, east to Panhandle, Texas, then west again to Albuquerque, New Mexico. He's an easy fella to travel with. He never needs bathroom stops. He doesn't care where we eat. And he stays awake with me all night. I'm sorry to see him go, but this week the company is sending me east, to Wauchula, Florida.

                  Trucking along—
                  Bobbi Jo

Raymond Johnson
111 Stony Lane
Rock Hill, SC 29730

June 28
Rock Hill, SC

Dear Tameka,
 I've had no word from Oliver in seventeen days. I'm starting to worry. What if he is lost? Please call me if he turns up at your house.

Love,
Uncle Ray

July 1
Redcrest, CA

Dear Uncle Ray,
   No word from Oliver. Are you sure
he's really coming?
   I still wish we could see you. I
asked Mama if we could come visit,
but she said it costs too much.
Daddy says he can't take off work
that long. Ever since I asked, Mama
keeps looking at family photo albums.
When she sees your pictures, she
says, "My baby brother!"
                  Love,
                  Tameka
                  XOXOXOX

July 4
Salt Lake City, UT

Dear Raymond Johnson:
    My grandfather found Mr. Woodman
in the middle of the reservation in New
Mexico. Poor fella—a mouse was building
a nest in his backpack. We don't know how
he ended up way out there, and he's not
telling. Grandpa brought him to Utah to
join me in the Fourth of July parade. I got
so tired of smiling and waving at the
crowds, but Mr. Woodman's brave smile
inspired me.
    I just sent Mr. Woodman off with three
sisters. They looked like such nice old
ladies, so I know they'll take good care
of him.

                    With all my love—
                    Melissa Tso, Miss Utah

P. S. I've enclosed an autographed picture.

July 27

en route to San Francisco, CA

Dear Mr. Johnson:

My sisters and I had the distinct pleasure of entertaining Mr. Oliver K. Woodman for the past 23 days. You see, we've lived in Kokomo, Indiana, all our lives. Until now, we'd never been west of the Mississippi River. Our dear papa died in January and left us an inheritance. We decided to use the money to tour the West this year. While in Salt Lake City, we saw Mr. Oliver in a parade, and after talking it over, we voted to give him a ride.

We stopped at a rodeo in Eureka, Nevada, where Mr. Oliver met an old friend named Bert. They had a moving reunion. Agnes, my oldest sister, insisted we show Mr. Oliver the great city of Reno. Mr. Oliver's advice was very helpful. We won $5,000!

We are heading south to San Francisco to see the Golden Gate Bridge, so we left Mr. Oliver yesterday in Rough and Ready, California. He should be at Miss Tameka's soon.

The Claremont Sisters
Agnes, Maggie, and Lucinda

P.S. We had afternoon tea every day. Mr. Oliver has the loveliest manners.

July 28
TO: Raymond Johnson
RE: Mr. Oliver K. Woodman

　Our family, currently on vacation, picked
up the above-named person in what I thought
was a misguided goodwill gesture. Little
did I know how lucky that gesture would be.
　Last night, we pitched tents in the
redwood forest. I woke at 3:00 a.m. to
screams of terror. Bears! Your friend
managed to frighten them away. He saved
our lives.
　With the deepest and most sincere
gratitude, we intend to deliver him to the
doorstep of Tameka Schwartz within the
next two days.

Gratefully yours,
Bernard Grape, Attorney-at-Law

Raymond Johnson
111 Stony Lane
Rock Hill, SC
29730

August 1
Redcrest, CA

Dear Uncle Ray,
   Guess who came to dinner? Oliver!
   He is so much fun! We are camping
in the backyard tonight. I hear he's
not scared of anything, so I'm glad
he'll be there. Tomorrow, at the
river, I'll let him hold my fishing pole
while I swim.
   Guess what else? Daddy and Mama
talked it over. We're coming to YOUR
house next month, and we'll bring
Oliver home. Isn't it wonderful?
                              Love, Tameka
                              XOXOXOX

P. S. Knock, knock. Who's there? Olive.
Olive who? Olive both you and Oliver!

ROCK HILL CITY NEWS
SEPTEMBER 15

# TICKER-TAPE PARADE FOR HOMETOWN BOY

*by Demetrius Dickson*

Oliver K. Woodman will return home today amid national acclaim for his cross-country journey. Woodman began his trip on June 1, in Rock Hill, South Carolina, and arrived in Redcrest, California, on August 1. The Rock Hill City Council announced that a ticker-tape parade to honor Woodman will be held today at 10:00 A.M., starting at the corner of Main Street and Cherry Road and proceeding down Cherry Road to Cherry Park.

Raymond Johnson and Tameka Schwartz, friends of Mr. Woodman, will host a picnic in his honor at Cherry Park at noon. At 1:00 P.M., Mr. Woodman will show postcards and mementos from his trip. The public is invited.

Oliver's Journey

Redcrest, CA
Rough and
Ready, CA
Reno, NV
Eureka, NV
Salt Lake City, UT
San Francisco, CA
Albuquerque, NM
Oklahoma City, OK
Panhandle, TX
Amarillo, TX
Fort Smith, AR
Dallas, TX

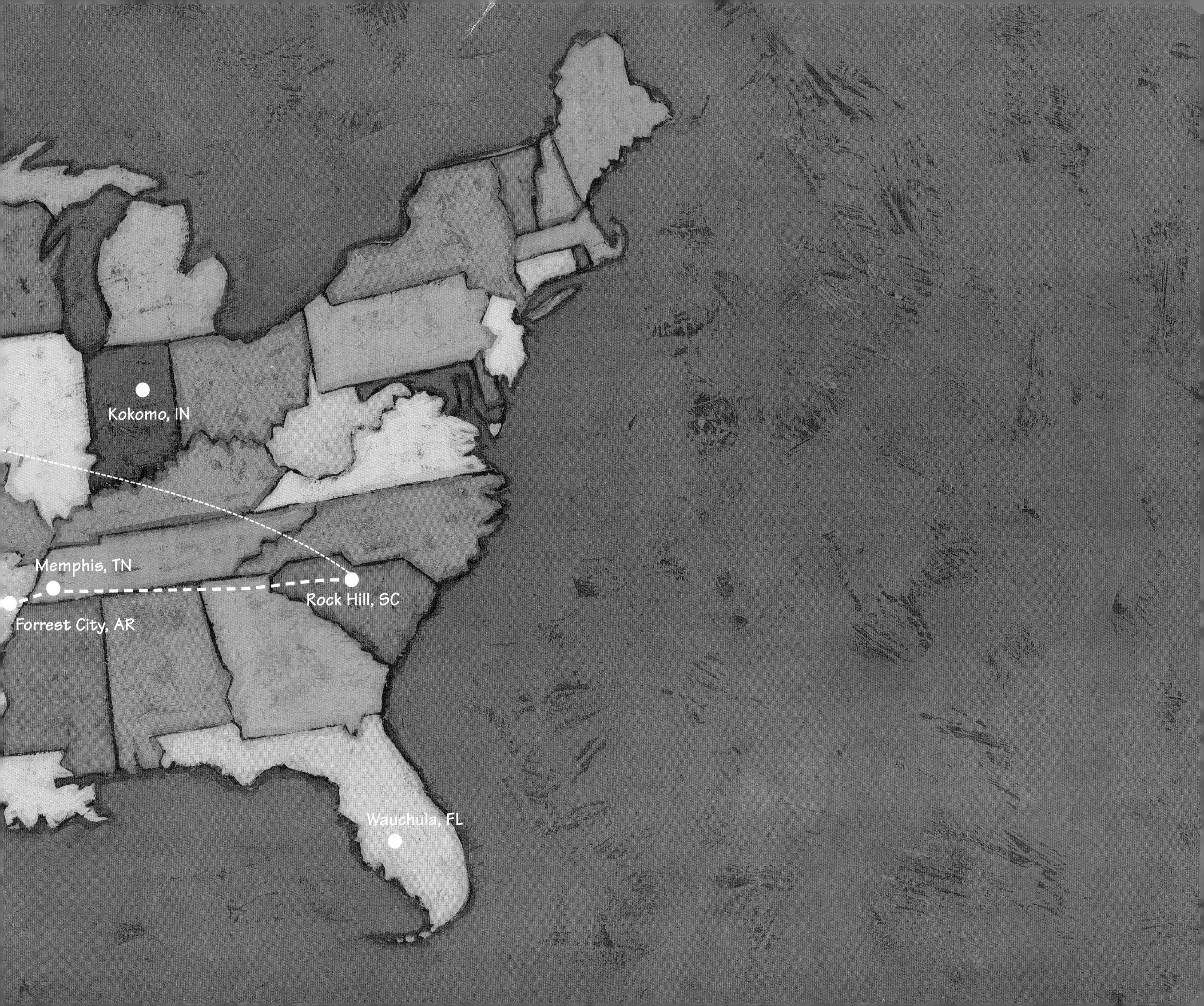

Kokomo, IN
Memphis, TN
Rock Hill, SC
Forrest City, AR
Wauchula, FL